JOSHUA'S MASAI MASK

Written by **DAKARI HRU**

Illustrated by **ANNA RICH**

LEE & LOW BOOKS Inc. • *New York*

Text copyright © 1993 by Dakari Hru
Illustrations copyright © 1993 by Anna Rich
LEE & LOW BOOKS Inc., 95 Madison Avenue, New York, NY 10016

Printed in Hong Kong by South China Printing Co. (1988) Ltd.
Book Design by Christy Hale
Book Production by Our House
The text is set in Goudy Sans Medium
The illustrations are rendered in acrylic on canvas
10 9 8 7 6 5 4 3
First Edition

_____

Library of Congress Cataloging-in-Publication Data
Hru, Dakari
Joshua's Masai Mask/written by Dakari Hru; illustrated by Anna Rich
p. cm.
Summary: Fearing that his classmates will ridicule his playing the kalimba in the
school talent show, Joshua uses a magical Masai mask to transform himself into
different people he thinks are more interesting, before realizing that his own
identity is one of value.
ISBN 1-880000-32-6 (paperback)
[1. Afro-American—Fiction. 2. Talent shows—Fiction. 3. Identity—Fiction.
4. Magic—Fiction]
I. Rich, Anna, ill. II. Title
PZ7.H85614Jo 1993
(Fic)—dc20 92-73219 CIP AC

Joshua loved it when Uncle Zambezi taught him to play the kalimba. He loved the feel of the wood, the rich chords, and the soulful rhythms.

But then he made the mistake of mentioning the school talent show, and the whole family jumped on him.

"Show them what you and that kalimba can do!" Uncle Zambezi urged.

"That's a great idea!" his mother said.

"I know you'll win!" His father beamed. And so he hadn't really had a choice but to sign up with his kalimba for the show.

But it was a terrible idea. Joshua's classmates liked rap. They liked kids like Kareem Cooper and Shamika Shabazz, who could dance like people in music videos. They'd think his kalimba was stupid. They'd laugh.

And sure enough, when Joshua walked into the auditorium for rehearsal, Kareem was onstage and the kids were cheering, "Go, Kareem! Go, Kareem!" Kareem snapped his fingers and boogied all around. His friend Shamika was as cool as the ice cream cone in her hand, spinning the records and scratching them in rhythm.

When they finished, the kids clapped and cheered and whistled. Then Kareem and Shamika sat down and everyone looked at Joshua.

"Look at that!" one girl said, pointing at Joshua's kalimba.

"Hey, whatcha got there? Show and tell? Something from your crazy uncle?" The kids laughed.

"It's nothing," Joshua mumbled. He got up to leave, fumbling for his jacket. At the door Joshua looked over his shoulder and saw everyone congratulating Kareem and Shamika. No way could his kalimba compete. He pushed open the door and walked home all by himself.

On his way, he stopped by his Uncle Zambezi's art gallery and told him what had happened. Uncle Zambezi listened, then he went into a back room and came out with three boxes. In the first was a brightly patterned dashiki. In the second box was a beautiful, new hand-carved kalimba. And in the third was a big ostrich feather mask from the Masai tribe of Kenya. Joshua fingered the feathers gently.

"Maybe you just need to get into the spirit of the thing. Give 'em attitude," said Uncle Zambezi. "When you go to the talent show, play your new kalimba, wear the dashiki, and bring the Masai mask. But be careful with it. The mask will listen to everything you say, and you must be careful to speak wisely."

Joshua just nodded and took everything home.

But no matter what his uncle said, the talent show was still tomorrow, and he was dreading it. Joshua wished he could just stay home, where no one would think he was crazy.

The next morning, Joshua tried on the mask and looked at himself in the mirror. "Be careful," he told himself in a low voice. Then he stuck out his tongue. "Who cares. I don't even want this silly mask, I just want to be Kareem Cooper."

Joshua shrugged and took off the mask. But when he looked in the mirror, what he saw made him choke.

It was Kareem's face!
He was Kareem!
And he was in Kareem's house.

He walked down the hall to the bathroom to get ready for his big day at the talent show. This was great. He looked so good, the kids would cheer him on and think that he was the best.

"Kareem, move your dumb face out of my way!" A girl who must have been Kareem's sister jabbed him with her elbow and slammed the door in his face.

He went downstairs to get some breakfast, but the refrigerator was empty.

"What do you think you're looking at?" Kareem's father barked. "You think food just gets in there all by itself? If you weren't so lazy, you might stop combing your hair for a minute and help out around the house. Who do you think you are, Righteous Rapper or something?"

Kareem couldn't stand any more yelling. He ran out of the house to think. Being Kareem wasn't as much fun as he thought it would be. But he still wanted to make a splash at the talent show. He thought about Kareem's father saying, "Who do you think you are, Righteous Rapper?"

Righteous Rapper! That would be the greatest talent show act ever! He touched his face, and the mask appeared again. Then in a flash he was Righteous Rapper. He was dressed in a red jogging suit, a red cap turned backwards, jewelry, sneakers and dark glasses. He felt great.

As he started down the street, some kids from his school spotted him. This is going to be hot, Righteous Rapper thought.

Then one girl screamed, "Righteous Rapper is here! Let's get his autograph!" One boy yelled, "I want his glasses and T-shirt!" Someone even yelled, "I want his pants!" And in a flash, a crowd of kids was bearing down on him like a runaway car.

Righteous Rapper beat it down 125th Street and ducked into a parking lot to catch his breath.

As Righteous Rapper, he would never make it to the talent show in one piece. What he needed to be was someone the kids would all respect.

He knew. The mayor! Righteous Rapper touched his face and the mask appeared again. He said, "I want to be the mayor."

And in a flash, he was.

As he walked toward the school, the kids made a path and asked to shake his hand.

"Are you coming to the talent show, Mr. Mayor?" they asked. "Wait till you see Kareem and Shamika." "We love you, Mr. Mayor."

It felt good.

Parents were streaming toward the school too, and the Mayor spotted Joshua's parents with Uncle Zambezi. "Hello, folks. Coming to see some talent?" he asked them.

"Oh yes, Mr. Mayor," his mother said. "Our son plays the kalimba."

"We're very proud of him," said his father.

The mayor swallowed hard and went inside to watch the show. He could hardly pay attention during the first acts because he felt guilty about disappointing his parents. But when Kareem and Shamika went onstage, the crowd got worked up.

Shamika held her blackberry ice cream cone and scratched the record. Kareem got carried away and did a big, wild spin. But in the middle of all that, Shamika's ice cream fell right on the record player and jammed it. The music stopped. Kareem fell flat on his back. The kids yelled, "We want a show, we want a show!"

The mayor thought, What can we do without music? Then he had an idea. He looked in the audience for his parents, then he ran backstage and touched his face.

Concentrating hard, he said, "I want to be Joshua and play the kalimba. I want to be me!"

In a flash, there he was in front of the microphone, the kalimba in his hands. Slowly at first, but then with confidence, he played:

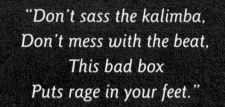

"Don't sass the kalimba,
Don't mess with the beat,
This bad box
Puts rage in your feet."

The audience listened. Kareem started dancing again.
Shamika joined in. Soon the rage was in everybody's feet.
Joshua's classmates danced and roared. The audience was cheering,
"Go, Joshua! Go, Joshua!"

Joshua looked at his Uncle Zambezi. From now on, that mask
would hang on Joshua's bedroom wall and not on Joshua. But the
kalimba would stay in Joshua's hands and the rage would stay in
his feet!

AUTHOR'S NOTE

In this story, the **Masai mask** that Joshua wears gives him magical powers. In real life, the mask has its own special meaning to the Masai people. Numbering over 240,000, the Masai live in Kenya and Tanzania in East Africa. The mask is an ornament an adult warrior wears when he goes to war. It is made of ostrich feathers tied onto a wooden frame. It is first worn when a Masai boy reaches the age of twelve to fifteen, as he participates in the rituals and ceremonies that initiate him into adulthood. During this period, he hunts for ostriches and birds, and wears the headdress as a symbol that he is a young warrior.

The **kalimba** that Joshua plays is a musical instrument used in certain regions of Africa such as Zambia, Nigeria, and Zimbabwe. It has a number of keys, usually made of metal or reeds, fastened over a bridge to a hardwood soundboard. The soundboard is held with both hands and the keys are plucked with the thumbs and sometimes with the index fingers.

Like drums, the kalimba is used in religious ceremonies by priests, healers, diviners, and rainmakers. It is also played at times of initiation, circumcision, childbirth, and for pure entertainment. I hope readers of this story will have the pleasure of hearing a real kalimba played out loud.